The New Adventures of Postman Pat

Postman Pat™

follows a trail

John Cunliffe

Illustrated by Stuart Trotter

from the original television designs by **Ivor Wood**

Hodder
Children's
Books

a division of Hodder Headline plc

More Postman Pat adventures:

Postman Pat and the hole in the road
Postman Pat and the suit of armour
Postman Pat in a muddle
Postman Pat misses the show

First published 1996
by Hodder Children's Books,
a division of Hodder Headline plc,
338 Euston Road, London NW1 3BH

ISBN 0 340 678097
10 9 8 7 6 5 4 3 2 1

Printed in Italy.

Pat was out on his letter-trail in Greendale.

When he had delivered the village post, he stopped to empty the letterbox at the top of the hill.

"A few more for Mrs Goggins to sort out," said Pat.

But when he arrived at the post office, he had a surprise.
"Good morning Mrs Gog— Oh, oh dear . . .
she's busy sorting something else out!"
Mrs Goggins had a tangle of string all looped and twined
and twisted round her hands.
"Drat this string—" she said, pulling and tugging at it.
It seemed to get worse, the more she tried.

"Now then, Mrs Goggins," said Pat, "don't get in a tizzy with it. You just want to take it slowly. Once you find the end - well, it *must* have an end - there are two ends to every piece of string . . ."

Pat's helping didn't seem to work any better.

"Dear me," he said, "it does seem to be in a mess, and I don't seem to have the knack. Perhaps you should try knitting it! Well, I'd better be on my way with the letters. *They're* not tangled, I hope. Good luck!"

Pat and Jess were on their way along the winding country lanes.
Up a hill and round a bend, Pat jammed his brakes on.

"What's that? Hold tight, Jess! A piece of string across the road?
Whatever can it be doing here? I hope it's not the end of Mrs Goggins'
tangle!"

Pat got out of the van to take a closer look.

"We'd better wind it up," he said to Jess, "before anybody gets
tangled up in it. Look, it goes right over this wall!"

Pat began to wind the string into a ball, as he followed it across
the road, over the wall, and into the field. Jess thought it was a ball
of knitting wool for him to play with. Pat put it down on top of the
wall as he was climbing over. Jess gave it a good biff with his paw.

"Stop it, Jess! We're not playing cat's cradle now," said Pat. "I think we'd better see where it goes to. It must be a very long piece of string. Come on, Jess, it looks like being a good walk."

Pat climbed a small hill, winding string as he went. Jess disappeared into the long grass. Just when Pat thought he had lost his cat, there he was, in front of him, sitting on a tussock of grass.

There was a scarecrow in the middle of the next field, holding the string for Pat.

"Please can I have my string, Mr Scarecrow?" said Pat.

But the scarecrow didn't want to let go of it! Pat pulled and tugged. He turned the scarecrow round and round. He held it upside down and shook it. It would *not* let go! Then, all at once, its head and legs fell off -

"Oh, dear, this silly scarecrow!" said Pat - and the string was free. It took Pat a long time to put the scarecrow back together again.

Then Pat was off once more, across the field, winding away at the string.

The mud sucked and slurped at Pat's feet, and splashed and sploshed all over his legs. They came to another wall. The string still went on. Pat jumped over the wall, straight into a gorse bush.

"Ooops! Ouch! Ooooh, *prickles*!"

Poor Pat, what a mess he was getting into. He said,

"I'll find out where this string goes to, if it's the last thing I do!"

On they went. Up another hill, and through a very wet
and sticky bog.

Now Jess had disappeared again!

Pat called and called. "Jess! Jess! Where are you, Jess?"

Then there Jess was, sitting on a stone, washing his paws!

"Jess! How did you get in front of me?"

Pat sat down on a nice dry stone, next to Jess.

"I'll just get my puff back . . . Now, Jess, don't go
disappearing again. It can't go on for ever. It's what I said to
Mrs Goggins: every string has an end *somewhere*."

On they went. Jess was soon far ahead of Pat once more.
Pat came to another road, then there was a garden wall.
"Now, whose garden is this?" said Pat. "I'm sure I've been here
before! Oh, I know, it's Granny Dryden's. How did we get here?"
The string went across the garden, through two flowerbeds,
three times round the sundial, then wound itself round and round
the washing-line. Granny Dryden was trying to sort it out.

"Who in the world has done this?" she said.

"Hello, can I help?" said Pat.

"Hello, Pat, I never heard your van. Just look at this mess. Have you got some letters for me?"

"Yes - but - no, I haven't got my van, I came with this string . . ."

"Came with this string?"

"Not with it, following it. Oh, it's all a muddle."

"It certainly is, Pat, and it's made a right old mess of my washing-line."

"It's not *my* string, but don't worry,
I'll sort it out for you," said Pat.
"It's just a matter of finding the end,
and then - oops - under there - then -
oh dear . . ."

"Are you sure you can do it, Pat?"

Pat was not sure at all. There
was more string wound round Pat
than anywhere else, and his ball
of string had rolled away under
a gooseberry bush.

"Now you know what it feels
like to be a parcel!" said Granny
Dryden. Somehow, Pat shook
himself free, and got the string
away from the washing-line.

"Now, that's a bit more like it."

Pat was off again, winding string like mad,
across Granny Dryden's garden, round the well,
over the potato patch, over the wall,
and into thick bushes and trees.

Jess popped up again, just ahead of Pat.
"We're off into the jungle now, Jess. Look out for big cats."
As they pushed through the leaves, they came face to face
with a pair of sharp and curly horns!

"Help! What's that?"
"Baaa-aaaa," said the creature.

"Oh, it's only a sheep," said Pat.
"A field full of sheep! Have you seen my string?
Baa-baa black sheep, have you any string?"
The string seemed to wind in and out of the legs of the sheep,
as though they had been doing some kind of dance with it.
"Can you all stand still for a minute,
whilst I sort this out?" said Pat.

But the sheep would not stand still at all.
It took Pat ages to unwind the wool from the hooves and horns
of all those frisky sheep. At last, it was free. Pat said,
"Bye-bye black sheep, and white ones as well!"

Pat followed the string through a gap in the wall, and up another hill. Then he saw it going high up into the branches of a big tree.

"Well, there must be something special at the end of such a *very* long piece of string. Whatever can it be?" said Pat.

He heard someone crying.
"Who is that behind the tree?
Oh, goodness me, young Katy and Tom!
What are you doing here?
And what are you crying about?"
"It's our new super-kite, Pat!" said Katy.
"Stuck in the top of this tree," said Tom.
"We can't get it down," said Katy.
"And we've lost our string as well," said Tom.
"Here's your string," said Pat, "safe and sound.
And I'll find a way to get your kite, never fear,
so dry up those tears."

Pat pulled at the string, but the kite would not move.
"Hmmm, it does seem to be properly stuck. There's Peter,
ploughing that field. I wonder if he can help?   PETER! Hi! Peter!"
Peter Fogg was too busy ploughing to bother about a kite in a tree.

Just at that moment, Ted Glen came along in his lorry. Pat could see a ladder on the back, so he ran to the road, and flagged Ted down.

"Can we borrow your ladder for five minutes, to get a kite out of that tree, Ted?"

"Well, I can't stop long," said Ted. "I've got to mend Doctor Gilbertson's greenhouse before the frost gets at her tomatoes. Did you say a kite?"

"Yes, it won't take long."

"Is that young Katy and Tom? Is it their kite?"

"Yes."

"Right!"

Pat and Ted soon had that ladder
off the lorry and over the wall. Ted Glen said,
"I'll hold the ladder, Pat. Steady as you go."
Pat went wobbling up the ladder into the tree.
"Well bless me, there's the kite, and Jess as well!"
said Pat. "How did you get here, Jess?"
Miaoouwwwww! was all that Jess would say.
"Come on, Jess, don't be frightened.
Come on, I'll just carry you down,
then I'll come back for the kite."
Pat could almost reach Jess, but,
when he stretched his arms out towards him,
the silly cat backed away along the branch.

"Oh, Jess, don't do that - look out!"

Pat's arm caught the kite, and away it went,
swooping down to the ground.

Katy and Tom called up,

"Ooh, thanks, Pat!"

"Now get along home, you two," called Pat.
"Your mum will be wondering where you've got to."

"All right, Pat!" called Katy.

"Thanks, Pat!" called Tom. "Bye!"

"We've got the kite, but poor old Jess
is stuck up here now!" said Pat.
He could not reach Jess,
no matter what he did.

"Well I'll have to get a move on," said Ted. "Doctor Gilbertson will never forgive me if the frost gets to her tomatoes."

Pat came down the ladder, saying,

"Well, Jess got up the tree on his own, so I hope he can get down the way he went up."

"You don't need to bother about Jess!" said Ted. "He's already here, waiting for you!"

"Bless us all!" said Pat. "Has that cat got wings?"
No one ever knew how Jess had got down safely.
Ted waved goodbye.
"Thanks, Ted!" said Pat. "Good luck with the greenhouse!
Where is that cat now?"
But Jess was sitting on the wall, next to Pat.
"Hello, have you popped up again ? You get everywhere,
don't you, Jess."

Pat had to make his way back, all across the muddy fields, over the hills, and through the bushes, to find his van and deliver the letters. The only thing was - well, all the fields looked alike, and Pat didn't know which way to go, *and* Jess had disappeared again! What a time he had. He came to a road at long last, and saw a man walking along.

"Now that looks like somebody I know."

It was Mr Pringle!

"Hello Pat!" said Mr Pringle. "Just out for a walk, you know! Having a look at the flowers and the trees. Are you looking for your van?"

"Well, yes, I was just wondering –"

"Three fields that way, turn left at the boggy bit, don't go in the field with the bull in it, and you'll be there in a jiffy."

"Oh, thanks, Mr Pringle. Thanks. Bye!"

Pat was on his way. It seemed much further
than Mr Pringle had said. He came to a road.
It looked like one that Pat knew. There was no sign of his van,
but there was the hum of an engine coming round the corner.
Was it Sam Waldron's mobile shop? Yes, it was, and Sam
stopped to see why Pat was standing there, all alone.

"Hello Pat. Anything wrong?"

"Have you seen my van anywhere?"

"You can't have lost it, Pat! It's too big to lose!"

"I was following a trail."

"A trail?"

Pat told Sam the whole story. How Sam laughed!

"I'm calling at Greendale Farm in a few minutes," Sam said.
"I'll make sure the twins got home safely. Your van's just round that
corner. It's safe enough. Bye, Pat!"

"Bye, Sam, and thanks!"

Pat soon found his van. But where was Jess? There was no sign of him. Pat went to clean his shoes on the grass, and when he came back to the van, there Jess was, curled up in his basket, pretending to be asleep.

"How *did* you get there?" said Pat. "I never saw you creep in. Well, we'd better get these letters delivered before the frost gets at them. We don't want to be late for tea."

But Jess was dreaming of string-trails that led to mice,
and saucers of milk, and plates of fish . . .